For Dad — S.B.

Text and design copyright © 2001 by The Templar Company plc

Illustrations copyright © 2001 by Simon Bartram

CIP Data is available.

Published in the United States 2001 by Dutton Children's Books,

a division of Penguin Putnam Books for Young Readers

345 Hudson Street, New York, New York 10014

www.penguinputnam.com

Originally published in Great Britain 2001 by Templar Publishing,

an imprint of The Templar Company plc, Surrey

Typography by Mike Jolley

Printed in Belgium

First American Edition

10 9 8 7 6 5 4 3 2 1

ISBN 0-525-46713-0

TIM PRESTON

PUMPKIN MOON

ILLUSTRATED BY
SIMON BARTRAM

Dutton Children's Books

New York

October 31

It's Halloween.

Time to **trick**–

or treat?

Midnight comes....

It's party time!

And away they go...

through the woods...

over the highway...

into the city.

It's a pumpkin
moon!

Next morning...

Anything can happen under a pumpkin moon.